AUTHOR
Paul Drummond

ILLUSTRATIONS
Al Warner
www.sigmafineart.com

DESIGN
Sean Marks

ART DIRECTION
Paul Drummond, Al Warner, Sean Marks

PUBLISHED BY P.A.D PUBLISHING 2010

www.stanleygetsstuck.com

The wind whistled through the trees as thunder clapped and lightening flashed across the dark sky. His whole body shook from the cold as heavy rain dripped from his ears onto the brown muddy ground. He didn't know how long he had been here. It felt like hours. His legs were stuck in the thick tangled branches of a bush and he couldn't move much at all.

He looked up through the trees of the forest, hoping for a few shards of sunlight signalling the arrival of the dawn. The moon and stars were invisible behind thick, dark clouds.

He listened hard for the singing of birds, or perhaps the sound of some cheeky squirrels playing, chasing each other up and down tree trunks. He heard neither. Stanley had never felt so frightened or alone.

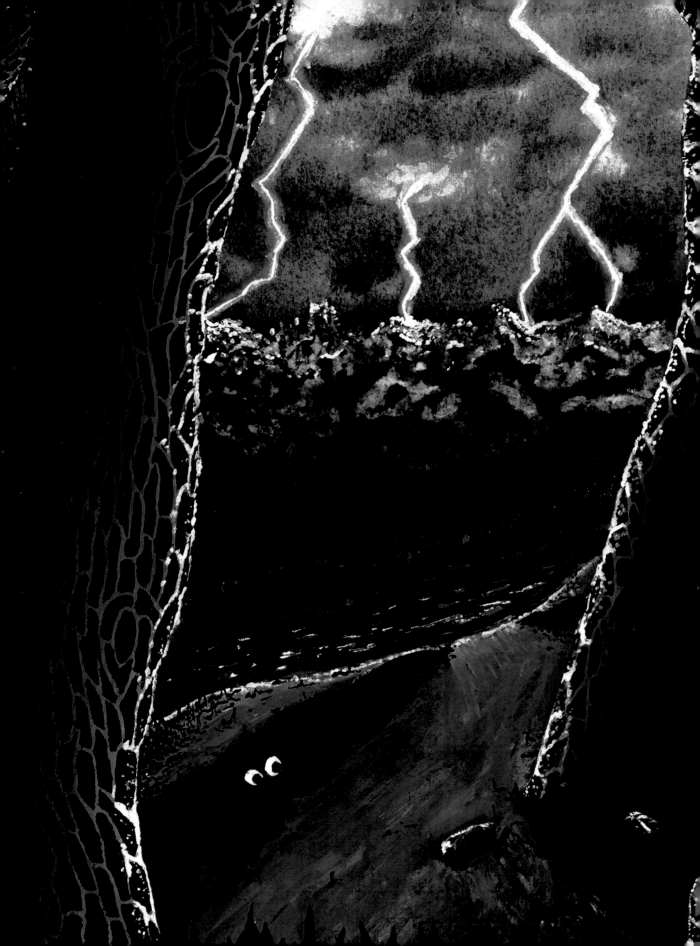

Stanley loved adventures. He lived in a small field on a hillside in a large flock of sheep. The other sheep spent their days eating grass, making fun of him, and when they were tired of doing that, they would simply ignore him.

They didn't like Stanley much because they said he was different. Unlike the other sheep in the flock who were all one colour, his white wool had big patches of black. The sheep said he looked more like a cow and laughed at him. This hurt Stanley's feelings and he often felt unhappy.

The only way to change this, he decided, was to leave and have an adventure! Perhaps he would even find some sheep that looked like him!

The next morning Stanley squeezed through a small hole in the bottom of a big thorny hedge near where the rabbits lived. He loved the rabbits because they would jump out of their holes any time he came near and play games; bouncing over him and running under him.

He would laugh as he watched them running, and then quickly changing directions, chasing each other for fun. On the other side of the hedge was a quiet road. Stanley took care to look both ways as he crossed, and made his way to a field on the other side.

He was so excited! The sun was shining, the weather was warm and, best of all, bouncing around in the distance he saw some sheep that looked just like he did: white with big patches of black!

As he got closer he noticed something a little different about these black and white sheep; the way they moved wasn't like any other sheep he had seen, but they certainly looked like him from here.

Something inside him told him to go the other way, but curiosity became too strong and so he decided to investigate! Stanley cautiously moved from bush to bush, keeping as close to the ground as he could. Closer and closer he crept until he peered through the bush closest to the black and white sheep. Something still didn't feel right.

He watched for a moment as they played with an old mattress that had been dumped in the field. *"Well, it's now or never!"* Stanley muttered to himself pushing his misgivings to one side. *"I'm going to say hi!"* But suddenly:

"Don't Move!" whispered a voice beside him.

Startled, Stanley looked down to see one of the small rabbits from the field. *"You scared me!"* exclaimed Stanley.

"Shush!" hissed the rabbit *"They will hear you!"*

"So?!" said Stanley, *"I was just about to say hi to them anyway! I have always wanted to meet sheep that looked like me."*

"They aren't sheep Stanley! Look closer! Look at their eyes! Look at their teeth! Look at their fur!"

Stanley looked harder, the teeth were sharp and the eyes were large. He looked really hard and saw that the patches of white wool on these creatures was actually the stuffing from the old mattress that they were playing with!

"WOLVES!" squeaked Stanley as he moved backwards. One of the wolves turned around and looked right at the bush.

"Get out of here! They have spotted you!" urged the rabbit, *"QUICKLY!"*

Stanley turned and ran; however, he knew that he wouldn't be able to get back to the field before the wolves caught him, so he headed to the river just a short distance away.

Running, he could hear the sound of the wolves behind, their snarls growing louder and louder as they quickly caught up with him! *"Don't look back!"* he told himself, just as a hungry wolf snapped at his tail-hair, he took a brave leap into the river. The water covered his eyes and went in his ears: oh, it was so cold!

The wolves stood on the riverbank howling in anger – they had just missed out on a tasty meal! They followed the flowing of the river, as it carried Stanley downstream.

The water was too deep for his legs to touch the bottom of the riverbed, so he was forced to kick all four of them as hard as he could as he tried to stay afloat. This was tiring work: he began to feel worn out. Looking around he noticed an old branch floating towards him. He clung to it with all his strength, hoping that he would reach a place where the river slowed down so he could climb out.

After he had been floating for a while, Stanley lost sight of the wolves. The river widened and Stanley noticed some small animals drinking at the water's edge. He saw pretty butterflies dancing in and out of the flowers, which formed a beautiful multicoloured carpet on the bank. He closed his eyes, feeling so relieved that he had lost the wolves.

It began to grow cooler, and when Stanley opened his eyes again he noticed there were no fields any more and, instead, he was surrounded by tall trees with huge leafy branches.

The river came to a bend and Stanley floated to one side into some very shallow water. He was so pleased to have stopped. He struggled up the bank, and noticed the sky had become darker. He rolled on the grass to try and dry himself and he suddenly froze! He could hear snarling and howling, and in the distance he saw the wolves again! Instantly, his mouth grew dry and an icy pit of fear formed deep within his stomach.

He turned and ran the other way, deeper into the forest, faster and faster until he came to a huge, tangled bramble bush which he threw himself into, hoping that this time they hadn't heard him. That is how Stanley got stuck.

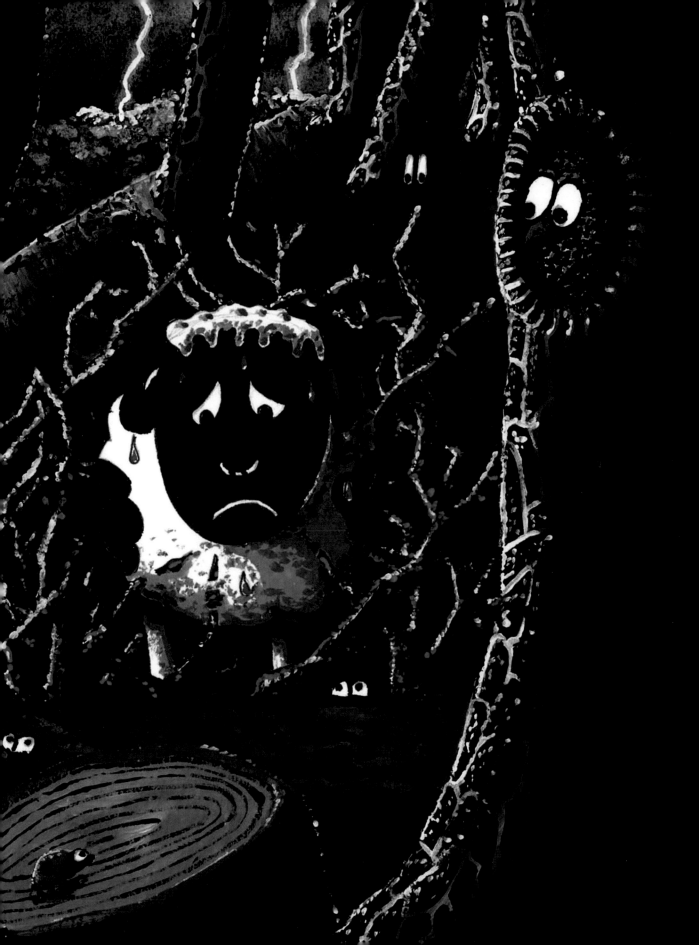

After many hours hiding in the bush, feeling frightened and cold, Stanley heard the sound of footsteps, and he saw the yellow glow of a light. *"Oh no!"* thought Stanley. He tried to back further into the bush, realising that he couldn't because his foot was stuck; and, as he moved, his leg twisted and he let out a loud *"BAAAAA!"*

He saw the outline of a man wearing a hooded cloak and he was holding a lamp. As he approached, he carefully parted the branches of the bush, looked at Stanley and smiled. Stanley looked away, wishing he could disappear! The man reached out his hand to stroke Stanley's nose, and began speaking in a calm, friendly voice.

As he did this, Stanley started to feel better. *"Look at you!"* said the man with a huge smile, carefully untangling Stanley's legs and picking him up and then gently laying him over his shoulders.

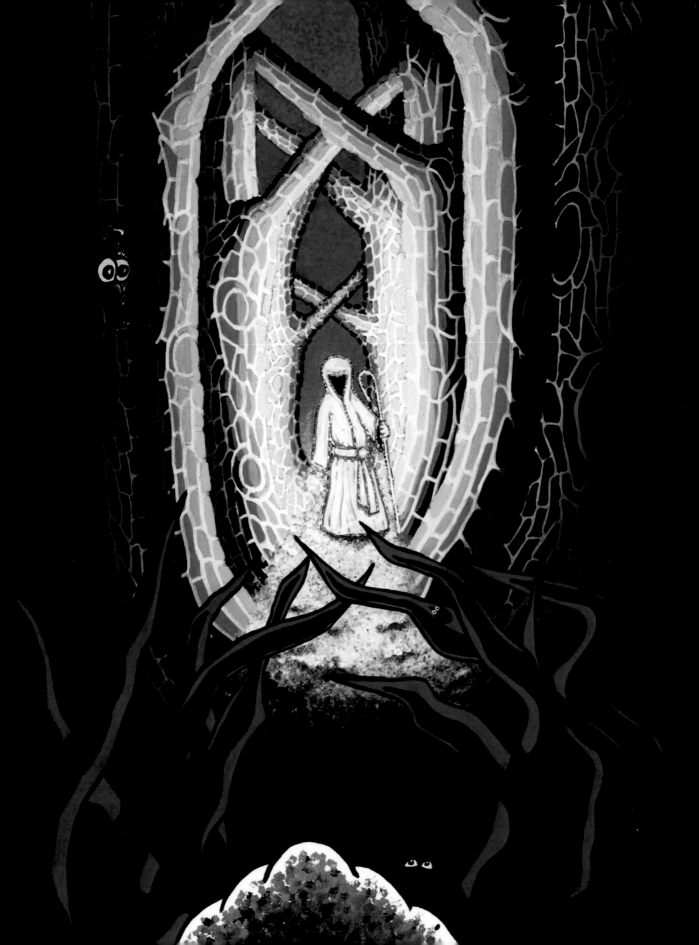

With Stanley snug on his shoulders, the man made his way through the trees and out of the forest. It was morning now. The sun was rising over the hills and the birds were singing as they awoke and searched for breakfast. Stanley was so tired that he couldn't keep his eyes from closing and fell into a deep sleep.

A while later, when he awoke, he saw that he was being carried toward a stony field with a small house next to it, and in the field were some sheep that he had never met before. Just the sight of them made him feel cross! None of the sheep looked like him! He just knew that these sheep would be horrible like those he ran away from: all because he was different.

The man put Stanley down onto the ground and
pushed him into the field. Stanley pushed back.
*"Come on now, you will be fine, don't be scared!
I am your shepherd and I will keep you safe."*
he said. Stanley ran to the opposite side of the
field, away from the other sheep.

He decided he wasn't going to speak to them,
so he sat on the floor with his back to them and
closed his eyes, wondering how long it would
take for him to be made fun of again.

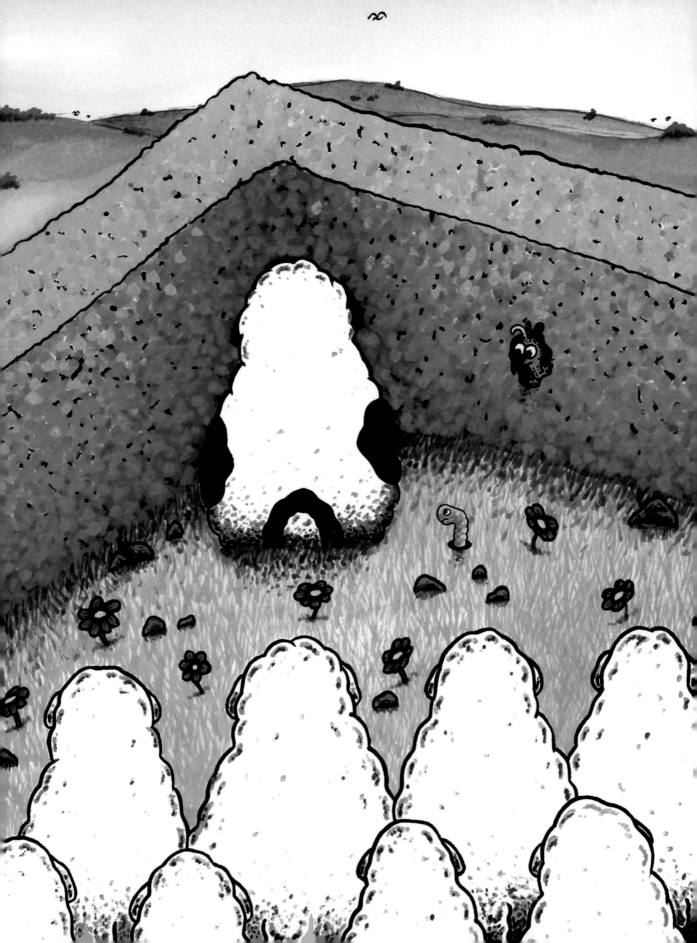

A little while later, he opened his eyes and turned around. He saw all the sheep standing silently behind him, smiling. *"What are you staring at?"* asked Stanley angrily.

"We just came to say hello!" said one of the sheep, in a cheerful voice. Stanley stared at them for a while longer, and to his surprise he began to smile too!

As the weeks rolled by, spring turned to summer, and the grass in the field became dry and brown. One evening the Shepherd came and told them that they would all be leaving in the morning for a field on the other side of the valley where there would be more food.

Stanley didn't sleep well that night. He really didn't want to leave this field. It was his home. He had become friends with the sheep, who had not made fun of him at all: instead, they had been kind and made him feel welcome.

He lay and worried about where they would be going. *"What if I don't like it? What if the Shepherd takes us the wrong way and we get lost? What if there are wolves up there?"* Many troubling thoughts went round and round in Stanley's head.

Early the next morning, just as the sun was rising, the Shepherd came to the field's gate with his usual smile, and led the sheep out onto the path. Stanley stayed at the back behind the other sheep kicking his feet on the dry, dusty earth. After walking for a while, they came to the top of a stony ridge.

The Shepherd made his way to the back of the flock to speak to Stanley. *"Keep up!"* he said *"We are going somewhere exciting! It's a beautiful field on the top of a hill with the sweetest, newest grass – it is better than anything you have ever seen."* He then pointed to the hill across the valley, showing Stanley where they were to go.

Stanley looked anxiously at the narrow dirt path that the Shepherd and his flock were approaching. He could see that it wound all the way around the valley, going back through the forest that he had become stuck in before. He then noticed a different road, a much wider, straight path which looked as if it headed down the valley and up the other side.

As he stood wondering why the Shepherd didn't take them this way instead, which seemed as if it was far easier and quicker, a little brown monkey lowered himself down from a signpost by his tail. *"Hi"* said the monkey, hanging upside down. *"My name is Scamp, what are you doing?"*

Looking up, Stanley replied *"Hi, I'm Stanley. I am deciding whether to follow the Shepherd down the narrow winding path to the other side of the valley, or whether I should take this wide road. It looks so much better!"*

"That's an easy choice!" said Scamp. *"Better is always best! I'm going that way to find my friends, so we can go together!"* Stanley agreed because the one thing he was certain of was: that if something looked good, it must be good! And plus, he would reach the new field before the other sheep!

Birds sang and bees danced busily in and out of the brightly coloured flowers that lined the wide road as Stanley and Scamp began to make their way toward the valley below. Scamp seemed friendly and good company.

Stanley learned that Scamp used to live in a circus, but that he and many other monkeys had escaped and now lived in the forest in the valley. They joked and laughed as they raced along in the warm sunshine, and Scamp entertained him with stories about life in the circus and the monkeys' exciting escape. He picked apples and performed tricks! It was so much fun!

After a while they reached a tall peach tree. Scamp quickly climbed up the tree and threw some peaches down onto the floor for them to play with.

As they were playing, Scamp noticed a skunk. He picked up a peach and threw it at the skunk, hard, laughing as it scuttled away. Stanley was surprised. *"Why did you do that?"*

"Because it's a skunk, nobody likes them, they stink!" Scamp replied. Stanley was puzzled – it seemed mean to treat any creature in this way - but he decided to join in because even though it felt wrong, it was sort of fun to kick peaches at the skunk and watch it run and dodge them.

Well, it was fun until the skunk grew angry and rushed towards them – Scamp managed to jump up into a tree and escape, but Stanley was still standing there as the skunk lifted up his tail and sprayed him with the most disgusting smelling spray.

Stanley was shocked! *"HEY!"* he shouted angrily at the skunk. As soon as he opened his mouth he realised it was a mistake as the foul spray engulfed him. Scamp laughed and laughed!

The sky became grey and thick clouds gathered overhead, and, sure enough, a few moments later heavy rain began to fall. Stanley was pleased because the rain washed away some of the foul skunk smell.

As they walked further, they noticed that the road stopped at an old wooden bridge across a wide green murky swamp that they had been unable to see from the top of the hill. Stanley felt happier as they walked onto the bridge. He stood and looked up at the hill where the new field was. Excitement rushed over him because he knew he would be there soon.

Stanley and Scamp slowly and carefully made their way across the creaking bridge. *"I bet this bridge breaks and we fall into the water with the crocodiles!"* Scamp joked.

"That's not funny Scamp! You shouldn't say things that you don't want to happen." They had almost reached the other side when there was a loud creaking sound from the wood and a huge SNAP! Suddenly the old bridge broke, sending them tumbling towards the bubbling swamp below.

In an instant Stanley felt a hard thump. Surprised, he opened his eyes and saw that he had landed on a large flat rock. As he looked around for Scamp, he saw the little brown monkey rising through the murky water beside the rock with a crocodile just behind him! *"CROCODILE!"* screamed Stanley, quickly reaching down and pulling Scamp out of harm's way just in time!

"That was close!" said Scamp, and with that, he jumped on Stanley's back, and stepped from his head onto an overhanging tree branch, and climbed up to the bank.

"I'm sorry Stanley" he called. *"I haven't got time to find someone to help you, I want to carry on and find my friends, if I don't leave now they might be gone. I'm sure someone will come by soon and help you!"*

Stanley watched as Scamp scampered away without looking back and he began to cry. *"I really thought Scamp was my friend!"* he cried, feeling angry, rejected and all alone.

"Why didn't I just follow the Shepherd like the other sheep did?" he sighed. Stanley was stuck again, and terrified; he felt so low that he decided if he did manage to get off this rock, somehow, he wouldn't go to find the others.

"I feel too ashamed to face the other sheep, and the Shepherd will be furious!" he thought, as a hungry crocodile stared at him. He felt that the Shepherd had given him a chance, and he had messed it up. *"It seems better isn't always best, if I don't know what better is to begin with!"* he said to himself.

As the sun dipped lower, sending pink, purple and orange streaks across the fading blue sky, Stanley saw someone approaching; it looked as if the figure was walking on the surface of the water towards him. *"I must be dreaming! This can't be real!"* Stanley exclaimed out loud. He blinked, rubbed his eyes, shook his head and looked again.

The figure was still there! He wasn't dreaming. What did this mean? People don't walk on water! As the figure came closer he recognised a familiar, gleaming smile and noticed that the crocodiles were all swimming away out of his path.

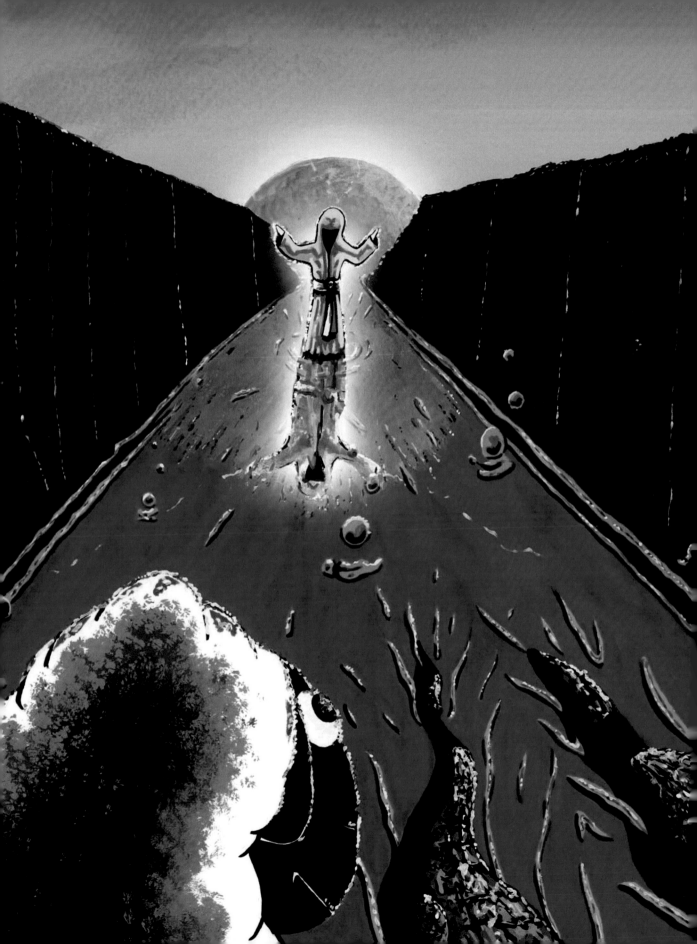

It was the Shepherd! Stanley's heart gave a leap of excitement and relief. As the Shepherd approached he called out to Stanley, *"Come on, little Guy, its time to take you home."* He lifted a sore, muddy, and smelly Stanley up from the rock and began to walk towards the opposite shore.

Stanley was amazed. He couldn't believe that the Shepherd could do this! The Shepherd looked at him and said: *"It's my job to take you the best way Stanley, and no matter how impossible things seem to you, or how lost you think you are, I can always reach you for nothing is impossible for me."*

After a long climb, they came to the top of the most beautiful hill. The sun was rising; illuminating the valley below. As they reached the gate some of the other sheep ran towards him. They were so pleased that he was safe, and made him feel so welcome. The grass was sweet and green, just like the Shepherd had promised; Stanley had never tasted such delicious grass!

Looking towards the far end of the field, he was surprised to see Scamp sitting on the other side of the fence, looking rather upset. He could see that his arm was limp. Stanley angrily turned his head away.

"After all Scamp has done to me, how dare he follow me here!" he thought. Then he remembered how many times the Shepherd had helped him. So he waved at Scamp and called him in.

Scamp awkwardly climbed over the fence and slowly walked towards Stanley and the other sheep with his head down. *"I'm sorry Stanley, I shouldn't have left you. As I searched for my friends I fell down a ditch and hurt my arm. When I found them, I couldn't climb and play so they didn't want me with them and they left me. Then I remembered how I behaved towards you. You really were a true friend to me, and I treated you badly. Please forgive me"*.

Stanley looked over and said *"I forgive you Scamp"*. As he did this, he felt the anger he had for Scamp begin to fade.

The Shepherd was sitting at the tree looking out into the distance. Stanley took Scamp over to him and showed the Shepherd his arm. The Shepherd instantly welcomed him with a hug. As he took Scamp's arm into his hand, Scamp regarded him with great admiration and curiosity. *"Who are you?"* he asked the Shepherd.

"I am The Good Shepherd." he replied, with a smile.